ROBBERS
AND
WITCHES

Judy Hindley
Illustrated by Toni Goffe

Kingfisher Books

Kingfisher Books, Grisewood & Dempsey Ltd,
Elsley House, 24-30 Great Titchfield Street,
London W1P 7AD

First published in 1993 by Kingfisher Books
2 4 6 8 10 9 7 5 3 1

The material in this edition
was previously published by Kingfisher Books in
My Own Fairy Story Book (1991)

BRITISH LIBRARY
CATALOGUING IN PUBLICATION DATA
A catalogue record for this book
is available from the British Library

ISBN 1 85697 037 X
Printed and bound in Hong Kong

CONTENTS

The Fairy Harp

Some robbers
had a bad day.

One stole
a shiny
chain,

but
a dog
came with it.

One stole
a money-box,

but
there was
nothing
in it.

One stole
a kettle,

but
it had
a hole.

Their fire went out.
"Oh, woe!"
cried
the robbers.

Everywhere they went,
something
stopped
them –
like a wall,
or a fence,
or a hedge.

That night,
as they rested,
they heard music.

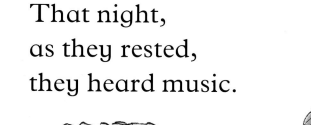

7

Fairies were singing
to a harp.
They sang,
"Magic harp,
play us away –
over walls,
under fences,
down the streams,
through the hedges."

And it did.

WHOOSH!

"Hurray!" cried the robbers.
"Just what we need!"
They grabbed the harp
and sang,
"Magic harp,
play us away –
over walls,
under fences,
down the streams,
through the hedges."

And it did.

WHOOSH!

WHOMP!

CRASH!

After that,
one became
a butcher,

one became
a pie-man,

and one learned
to do repairs
on pots and kettles.

It suited them
much,
MUCH
better.

12

The Magical Apple Tree

Rosy lived
with a mean old wicked witch.
The witch did nothing at all
but count her money.

Rosy did all the work.

She fed the hens
that laid eggs
for the witch.

She fed the cow
that gave milk
to the witch.

She fed the horse
that pulled the cart
that carried the wood
for the witch's fire.

All summer
she grew corn and hay and oats
to fill the barns
for the animals' winter food.

But the witch
sold the corn and hay and oats
and kept the money.

When winter came,
there was no food
in the barns.

The hens were so hungry
they laid no more eggs.

The cow was so hungry
it gave no more milk.

And the poor old horse
was too weak
to pull the cart.

The witch said,
"YOU'RE NO USE,
NOW."

Tomorrow morning
the hens will go
in the cooking pot
and the cow will go
to the butcher.
That old horse can go
wherever it likes –
and so can you!"

She kicked Rosy out
into the snow
and slammed the door.
Then she laughed
her wicked laugh,
"Caw, caw, caw!"
just like a mean old crow.

Rosy cried,
but the hungry animals
gathered around her.

So she said,
"I must go on.
After all, crying won't help,
and trying *might* help."
She picked up her empty basket
and went away
into the cold, bare woods.

Rosy walked and walked
till she came to
an apple tree.
It called to her.
In a sad, little voice
it cried,
"Please, dear Rosy,
shake me, shake me,
or this heavy fruit
will break me!"

Rosy looked up.
All she saw
was one dead leaf.
But the tree cried,
"Shake me, shake me!"
So she did.

Suddenly,
it was full of
yellow apples!
Rosy filled
her basket
and hurried home.

As she went,
the basket got
heavier and heavier.

But she didn't stop
for a minute
till she got home.

She tipped out the fruit
and the animals crowded around.

None of them saw
that the last five apples
had turned to gold.

But
the witch did.
"AHA!"
she cried.
"WHO
DID
YOU
ROB?"

"No one," said Rosy.
"I found these apples
in the woods.
There were lots and lots."

"LOTS?"
cried the witch.
And she rushed
into the woods.

Through the bare trees
the magical apple tree
glimmered with fruit.

But the witch
pushed past.

"Please," cried the apple tree,
"shake me, shake me,
or this heavy fruit
will break me!"

But the witch said,
"Pooh!
I'm looking for
golden apples.
Shake yourself!"

So it did.

But this time,
the apples
turned into stones.

"Ow, ow, ow!"
cried the witch,
just like
a mean
old crow.
She hopped
and flapped
just like
a mean
old crow.

And suddenly
the wind
picked her up
and whirled her away.

And she never came back.

But Rosy sold the golden apples
and was rich!
And she and the animals
never went hungry again.

What Do Witches Like?

What do witches
like to wear?

Big, black boots, big, black capes,
    big, black hats on their straggly hair!

What do witches like to eat?

Fat rats, boiled bats,
beetles, bugs and spider stew —
what a treat!

What do witches
like to do?

Read a
magic
spell
book,

yell a
wicked yell,

brew a
magic
potion,

cast a
wicked
spell,

28

dance a wicked witch dance
in a magic ring,

ZOOM
on a broom and

scare you!

BOO !

Also available in the **I CAN READ** *series*

Feathery Furry Tales
Giants and Princesses